For Louis and Freya
and anyone else who is a bit worried.
J.S.

For every child waiting for a new brother or sister
F.C.

First published in Great Britain in 2009 by
Gullane Children's Books
185 Fleet Street, London, EC4A 2HS
www.gullanebooks.com

1   3   5   7   9   10   8   6   4   2

Text © Jonathan Shipton 2009
Illustrations © Francesca Chessa 2009

A CIP record for this title is available from the British Library.

ISBN: 978-1-86233-719-0

Printed and bound in Indonesia

Baby Baby blah blah blah!

Jonathan Shipton

illustrated by
Francesca Chessa

GULLANE
CHILDREN'S BOOKS

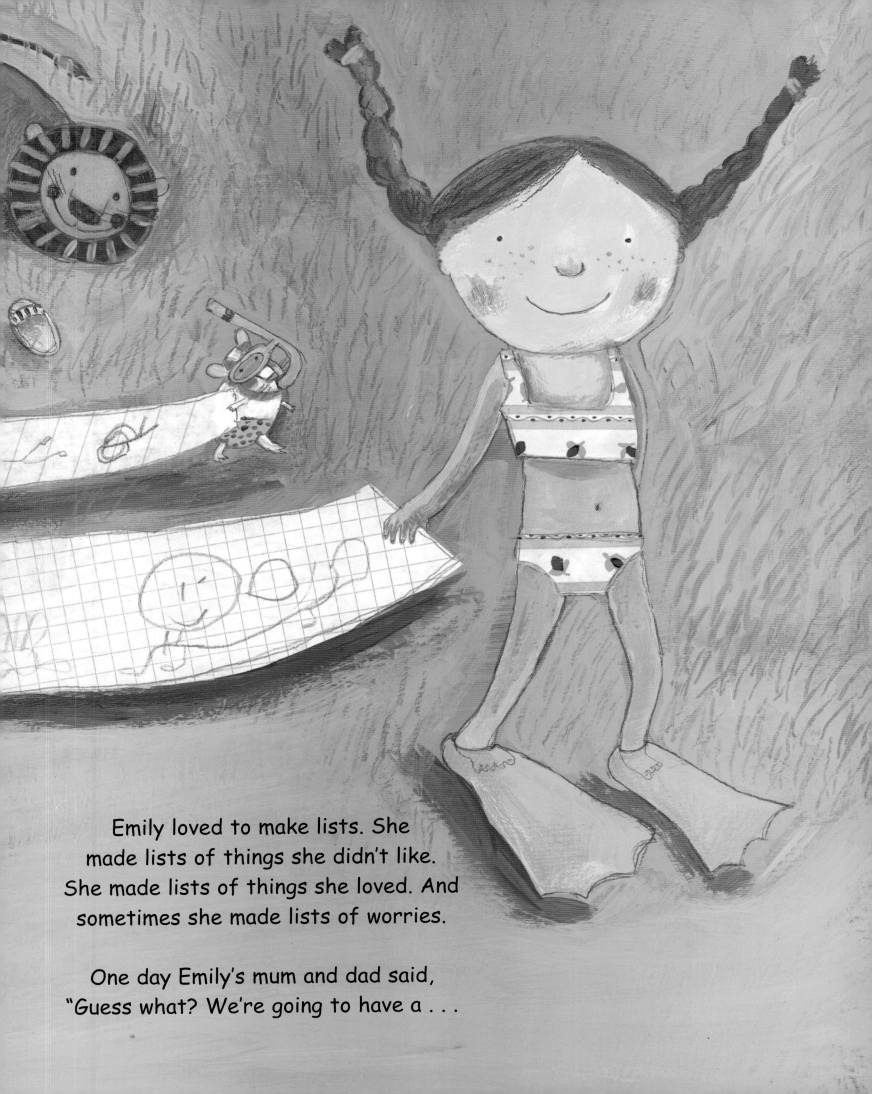

Emily loved to make lists. She
made lists of things she didn't like.
She made lists of things she loved. And
sometimes she made lists of worries.

One day Emily's mum and dad said,
"Guess what? We're going to have a . . .

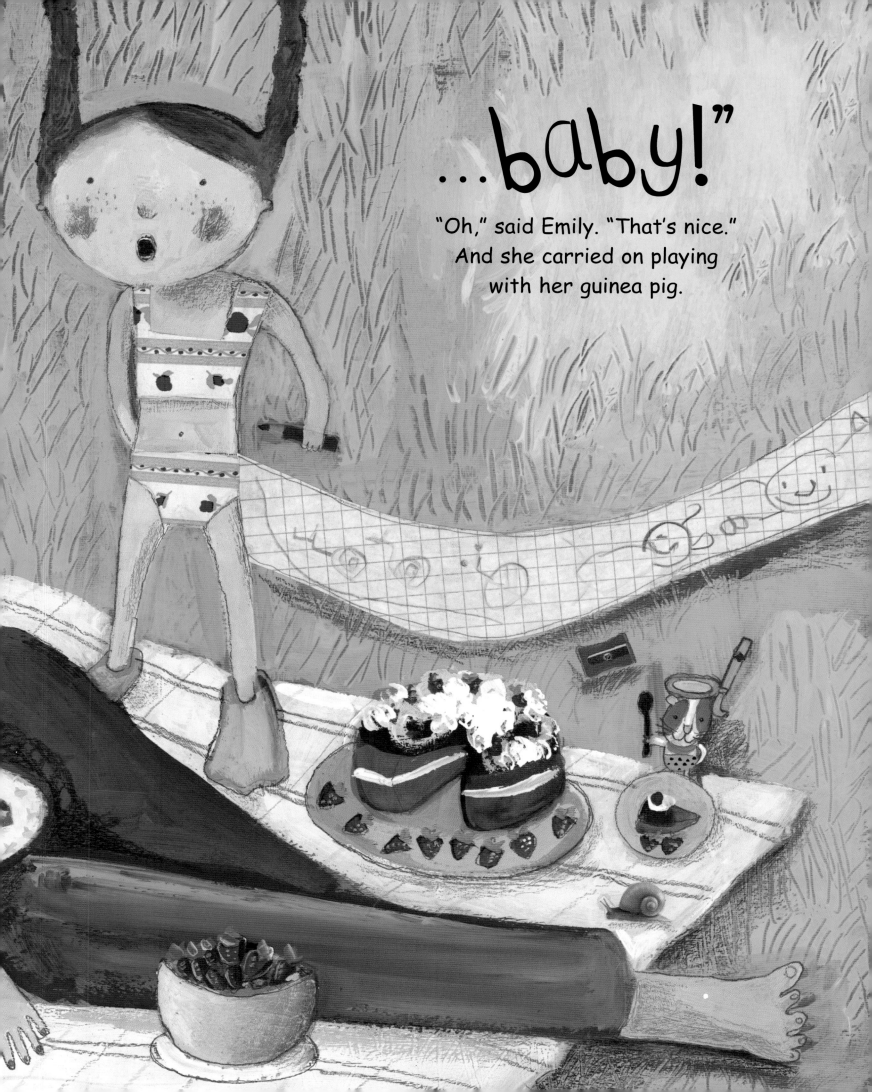

...baby!"

"Oh," said Emily. "That's nice."
And she carried on playing
with her guinea pig.

That night Emily said,
"You know this baby, is it going
to be a brother or a sister?"
"It's going to be a surprise," said Emily's dad.
"I'd like a sister baby," said Emily.
Emily's mum patted her round baby bump.
"We'll just have to wait and see, won't we?"

Well the baby bump grew. And a little worry started to grow in Emily's mind. And the bigger the baby bump grew, the bigger Emily's worry grew. One day the bump was so huge that Emily couldn't even fit on her mum's lap.

A bit later, Emily came into the kitchen.
"Guess what I've been doing," she said.
"Have you been making a list?" suggested Emily's dad.
"Yes I have," admitted Emily.
"Is it anything to do with babies?"
"Yes it is," said Emily.
"Good," said Emily's dad.
"It's not that good," warned Emily.
She settled the guinea pig on her lap and began to read.

A baby is good because....

It is really tiny.

Its head is soft and snuffly.

You can play pat-a-cake.

When it has grown a bit you can feed it all kinds of squish.

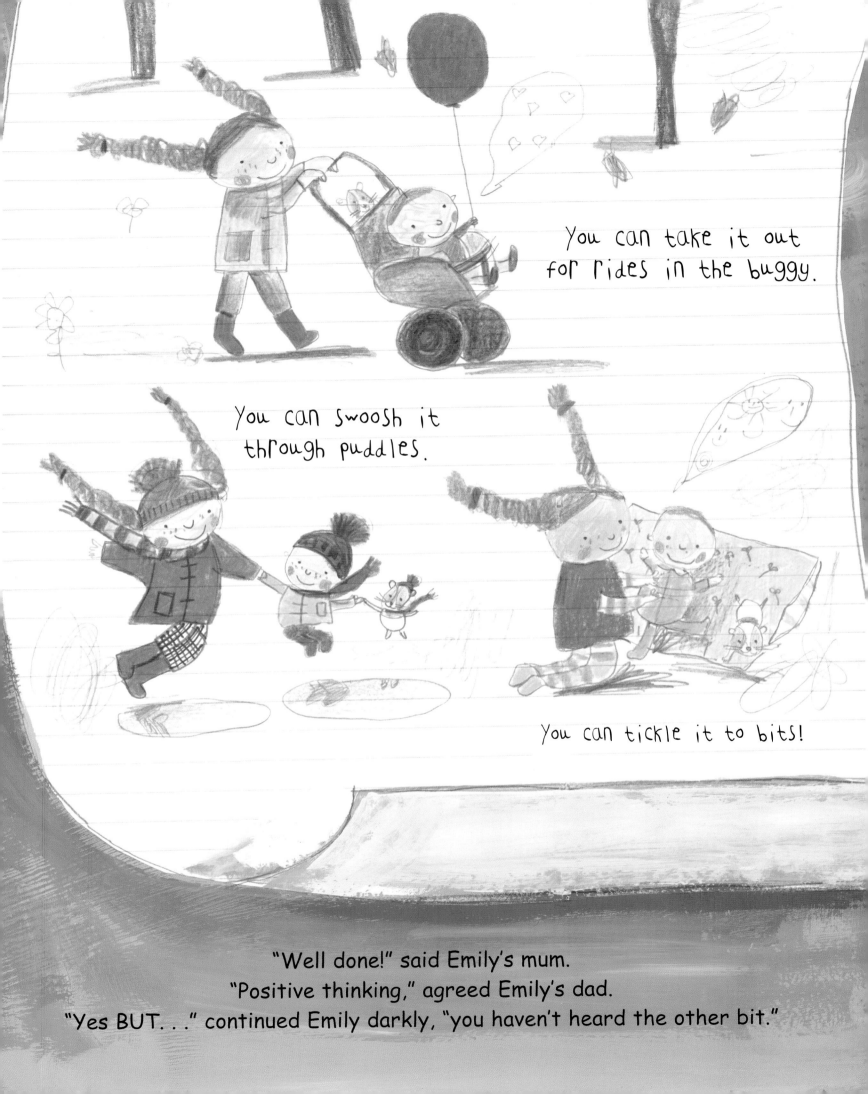

You can take it out for rides in the buggy.

You can swoosh it through puddles.

You can tickle it to bits!

"Well done!" said Emily's mum.
"Positive thinking," agreed Emily's dad.
"Yes BUT. . ." continued Emily darkly, "you haven't heard the other bit."

cry.

waaah!

It cries if it's hungry.

It cries if it's thirsty.

It cries if it's tired.

It cries if it's hot.

It cries if it wants to do a poo.

"But that's not the worst thing," said Emily. "When the baby comes . . .

. . . everyone will come rushing round. And it will be baby this and baby that and baby goo goo and baby blah blah blah. And I will have to eat left-over squish and go to school in a babygro and mittens. Everything will be upside down and inside out because that's the way it is when a baby comes into your house!"

"Oh dear," sighed Emily's mum. "That sounds awful."

"But it's not going to be like that," said Emily's dad. "Come and sit on my lap and I will tell you a story about a baby."
"See!" said Emily triumphantly. "It's already started!

Baby baby blah blah blah!"

"No!" interrupted Emily's dad.
"This story is about **YOU!** May I begin?"
Emily nodded.
"A long time ago there was just Mum and me. We did all kinds of stuff together: walking, dancing, climbing up mountains. We were so happy I couldn't imagine it being any better. But then guess what happened?"

"Me . . . ?" said Emily.
"Yes! But having you didn't stop us
doing things, we just took you along too!"
"Even up mountains?" said Emily suspiciously.
Emily's dad smiled. "Well, maybe not up mountains . . ."
"But we did go on bike rides together," said Emily's mum.
"And now we go skating together," said Emily.
"Exactly! It just gets better and better,
doesn't it?" said Emily's dad.

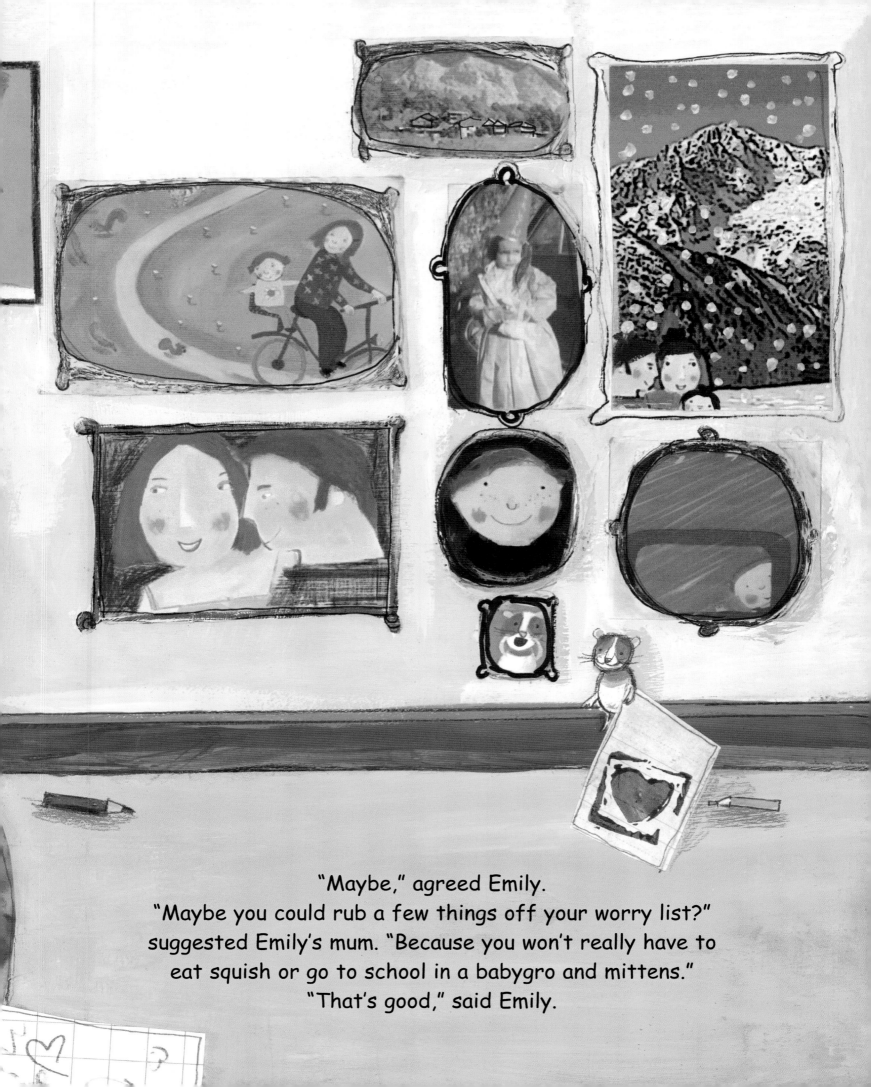

"Maybe," agreed Emily.
"Maybe you could rub a few things off your worry list?"
suggested Emily's mum. "Because you won't really have to
eat squish or go to school in a babygro and mittens."
"That's good," said Emily.

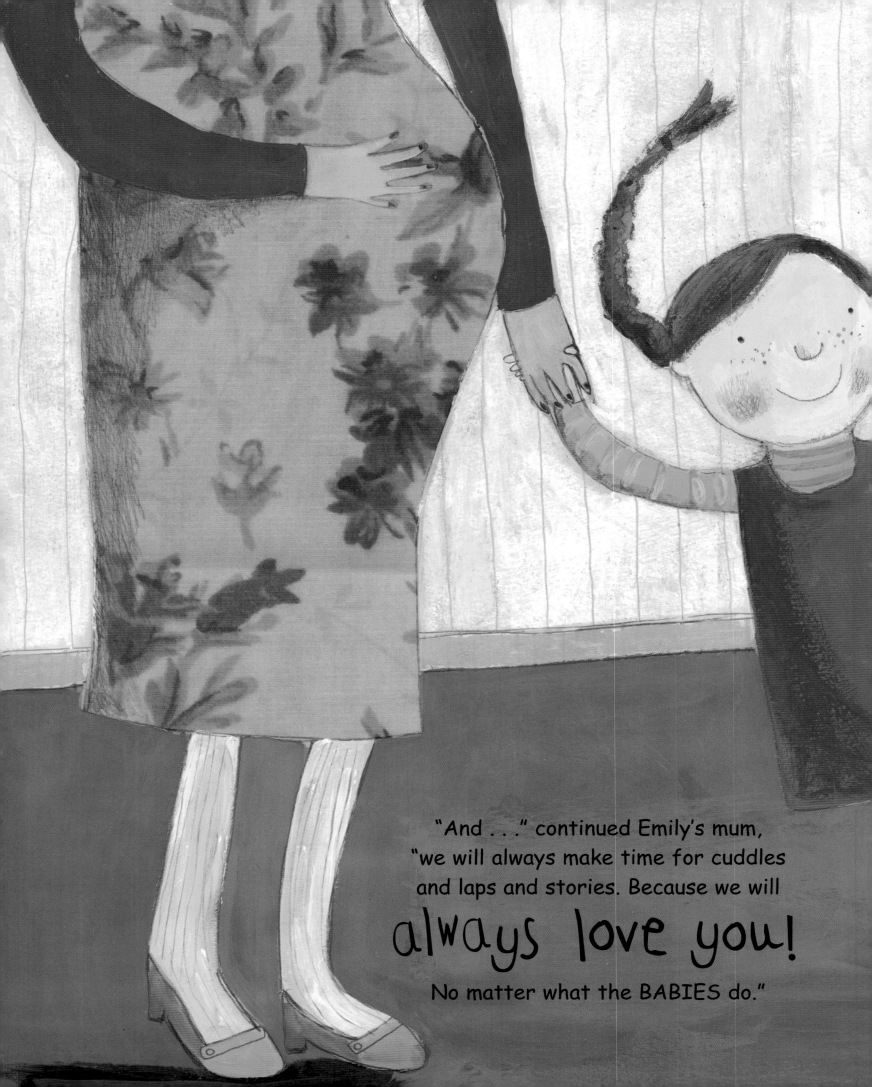

"And . . ." continued Emily's mum,
"we will always make time for cuddles
and laps and stories. Because we will

always love you!

No matter what the BABIES do."